CROCODILE ISLAND

By Barnabas McGrann

CONTENTS

CHAPTER ONE

HOLIDAY TIME

I'm Bobby McCain, a small boy aged 10. I live in a town called Barley. It's a pretty nice town at the moment but it's always being renovated, so when reading this book Barley will probably be very much better! This book is about the time the rest of the family and I went on holiday to Australia for a fortnight for my Uncle Jake's 27th birthday.

We got onto the plane - Easy Travelling Express - and found our seats. I was sat next to my cousin Ava - aged 11 - she was sat next to her Auntie Mollie - aged 10. Altogether there was;

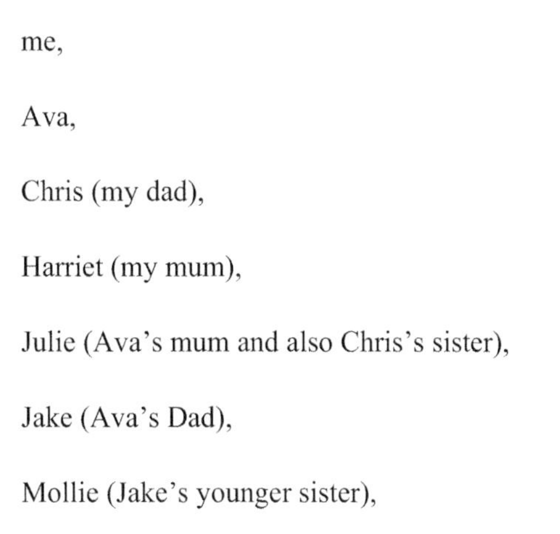

me,

Ava,

Chris (my dad),

Harriet (my mum),

Julie (Ava's mum and also Chris's sister),

Jake (Ava's Dad),

Mollie (Jake's younger sister),

McCain (Julie and Chris's Dad).

McCain was dumb, crazy, a kind of psychopath and had the most irritating way of saying "Hi". It sounds like "Huuy". McCain also had the same surname as his first name - McCain Martin McCain! McCain also wore a light grey wig that always fell off. He worked at the Barley Police Station.

There was also Snowball. She was Ava's dog, though on the plane, of course, she had to sit in a cage in the hold. Snowball was given to Ava's family as a 'thank you' present by my two older cousins Karl and Rebecca who lent out their caravanette to them. Ava's mum Julie looked after the caravanette so well that Karl and Rebecca thought they just had to get her and the rest of the family a big present, so they got them a beautiful husky dog!

Ava and I love animals with all our hearts (besides God) and we were extremely excited about going to Australia and hopefully seeing lots of wildlife! My favourite animal - the saltwater crocodile - lives exclusively in Australia and I was hoping to see one. So were Ava and Mollie.

It was some time in May. The plane was in take off position but wasn't moving yet. Suddenly the great plane engines let out a roar. Someone on board the plane screamed (possibly a child who has nothing to do with me or this book). The plane leapt forward, gaining speed fast. I wished I could have seen the plane's speedometer for I'm sure we were going about 500 miles per hour!

"My bones are at the back of my body!" cried Ava, shouting above the noise.

"So are mine!" I shouted.

"The world outside seems to fly by!" shouted Mollie who was sat next to the window.

"You mean we're flying by the world" I shouted, laughing.

With a great roar, the Easy Travelling Express lifted its heavy body off the ground and was in the air. We climbed steadily until we were above the clouds. Ava, Mollie and I were all holding our bellies as if we thought they were going to fly away!

I always wonder how a heavy metal machine can get into the sky and seem as light as a feather (probably lighter because it doesn't fall back down like a feather does) but it doesn't amaze me as much as how the poisonous dart frog doesn't take the deadly effects of its own sweat - which is the most deadly poison any animal can inflict!

Mollie said she could see the outside world getting smaller and smaller as we flew higher and higher. McCain, who was sat on a row of empty seats, was looking quite bewildered and I bet, if I had asked him, he probably wouldn't have even known we were on board a flying object!

Our plans were to get to Australia, find a shop that sold tents, buy some, go to a good out-of-the-way camping spot and have a lovely fortnight in Australia, then we'd give the tents to some homeless person who needed one and go back to the airport and fly all the way back home to Barley! Altogether - that's not exactly how it went.

We planned to find a nice billabong (an Australian word for 'watering hole') to camp near. We might have a good chance of finding a croc then (crocs live in billabongs) though if there wasn't one we could still paddle and swim in the water.

Nobody told Grandad McCain that we were on the hunt for man eating crocodiles, whew! He would probably jump out of the plane or something. Ava, Mollie and I...oh and Snowball (known as 'the fabulous four') were all mad (in a good way, though, not like McCain). We really enjoy being mad.

As the plane flew, a voice above me said "You can now take off your seatbelts - the toilets are open at the front and rear end of the plane". I clicked off my seatbelt and Ava and Mollie did the same. A door at the front of the plane was opened and out came a woman pushing a food trolley full of scrumptious foods. I had five pounds in my pocket and so I stopped the 'trolley pusher' and had a look at the food for sale; beef sandwich - no, roasted chicken - no, lamb limb - was everything here meat? I'm a vegetarian but also eat fish...so I'm a pescatarian. Chicken nuggets - nooo!

"Is there a vegetarian option, Miss?" I asked the trolley pusher.

"There's a a vegan option" she said and handed me a menu. I chose the first thing I saw - vegan nuggets. I knew exactly what they tasted like because they were sold back at Barley.

I gave the trolley pusher the menu and the money and she handed me the nuggets. Ava bought some vegan nuggets too. She was vegetarian like I thought I was. Mollie (who was neither vegetarian nor pescatarian) bought a bag of chicken strips. POOR CHICKENS!!!

CHAPTER TWO

ON THE PLANE

After the vegan nuggets snack I decided I would have (or try to have) a nap. I searched for the lever thingy that made the chair go back into a sleeping position and soon found it. I pulled it hard expecting it to be heavy. In fact it was very light and I pulled it right up. The chair shot forward and completely crushed me.

"What are you doing?" I heard Ava say between laughs.

"Trying to sleep" I said "This is a nightmare". I pushed the lever down and the chair shot back into an old sleeping man behind me. He was sat next to Aunt Julie, who was sat next to Uncle Jake, who was looking out of the window. He was in the middle of a rather important daydream and didn't notice the scenario next to him.

The old man awoke and looked disapprovingly at me.

"Are you trying to be funny young lad?" he said with a Cornish accent.

"No, sorry" I replied "I was just trying to put my seat back so I could have a nap but it shot back into you. Sorry - so sorry".

The old man leaned over and gently lifted the chair lever up. I jumped forward expecting the whole thing to crush me again but it didn't. The chair back-rest simply lifted a bit and stayed in an exceptionally good sleeping position.

"Thanks a bunch!" I said to the old man. He grinned and said "Anytime, anytime".

After half an hour of trying to get to sleep I gave it up. The plane was suffering from turbulence and it kept me awake. I fiddled around with the lever and managed to get the seat back into its original position. The old man with a Cornish accent was asleep again.

I bent over so I could see out of Mollie's window. The sun was setting...so was I - my seat was sweaty and I was beginning to slide off it. I got off the chair and wiped it with the sleeve of my light blue jumper, then I sat down again.

"Look!" cried Mollie "There's another plane!"

Ava and I tried to look but Mollie was in the way.

"It's gone" she said at last. Jake had seen it though.

"It looked like a private jet or something" he said.

We were on a four hour flight to Thailand. There we had to swap planes and take another seven hours to Australia - Dad said it would take two WHOLE days!

Finally, after ages of sitting in that same seat, a voice above me said "Please fasten your seatbelts - toilets on the plane are now locked". Then all throughout the plane was heard the tiny clicks of seatbelts going into their sockets.

It was dark outside and Mollie could see the lights of the runway we were about to land on. They were getting close very quickly. As we approached we all began holding our bellies again. This was actually the first time I'd ever been on a plane and I wasn't sure if the landing was going to be a success!

I heard Julie say to Jake behind me, "I hope all the wheels are greased properly". I began holding my belly harder than ever. I cannot think what my insides were up to.

I looked at Grandad sat by himself on the row of empty seats. He was asleep. He also didn't have his seatbelt fastened properly. It was all fastened behind him, not holding him to the chair. I didn't tell anyone - I wanted to see what would happen to him.

"Here we go!" I heard Mum cry. Suddenly with a big bump the plane hit the ground. I watched Grandad but he was just shaken a bit. He didn't wake up.

But then the plane bounced again and landed with an even bigger bump. This time Grandad was bounced right off his seat. The plane braked very suddenly and Grandad was flung to the front of the plane where he crashed through the locked toilet door. I always knew those toilet doors were not strong.

CHAPTER THREE

ARRIVAL

When the plane had stopped, Ava, Mollie, Julie and I went to the front to look for Grandad. We found him amidst the rubble of the toilet door he had crashed through. He didn't see us watching him as he shakily got to his feet. He lost his footing and slipped over with his head in the toilet. His hair/wig - as usual - fell off into the water. I couldn't help chuckling as I saw him reach out for support and grab the flush handle. He pulled it and the toilet flushed. The others and I left him to find that he'd flushed his hair/wig down the toilet.

We got off the plane and into the cool dark night air. The air smelt fresh as all holiday air smells.

"So this is Thailand!" I said. A voice behind me interrupted - it was Grandad.

"Guys!" he cried. Everyone looked around except Mum and Dad because they were getting something out of the small bag.

Grandad was running down the steps from the plane wearing his huge cowboy hat to cover up his baldness. He tripped up on his own feet and crashed down the tall stairs.

"My hair was flushed down the toilet!" he panted as the water from the toilet dripped off his head.

"Keep your hair on" grinned Ava.

"I would if I could" Grandad cried.

"I'm joking" laughed Ava.

"You'll have to wear that hat till we can get another wig" I said.

"Can't a grown up say something to me?" cried Grandad.

"I agree with Bobby" said Mum.

We had quite a long wait to pick up our suitcases and an even longer wait to pick up Snowball the dog.

Snowball greeted us with barks and licks.

"I bet she's got cramp" said Ava.

"Poor Snowball" I said.

"I hope she won't be too hot in Australia" said Mollie.

"Oh, she'll find a shady spot" said Ava.

Soon Snowball was packed into another plane alongside our big bags. We climbed aboard too and found our seats. I was sat next to the window this time!

The plane was soon off. I could see the Thailand moor at night - so I couldn't actually see it, just a few lights of houses here and there.

Once again I bought some vegan nuggets (which I now call 'vegan nug-nugs') from the trolley pusher and Ava and I shared and enjoyed them. Mollie was sleeping. It was about 4 in the morning so I couldn't blame her. After the vegan nug-nugs I decided to have a sleep myself. I shut the window shutter and lay back. There wasn't anyone behind me so I wasn't afraid of crushing them. This plane hadn't very bad turbulence and so I fell asleep fairly quickly.

I dreamt I was in Australia! There were crocodiles everywhere giving rides to children! I dreamt of the white Australian sand and the big golden sun! Suddenly a huge flying object crashed into the sea! I woke with a jump. When I realised that it was only a dream I called to Dad, "Dad, what's the time?"

"Nine o'clock" he said.

I opened my window shutter and the blinding golden sunlight flooded in! I waited for my eyes to adjust and when they did I saw the Australian Ocean. It didn't look like the sea in my dream - it looked miles better!

I couldn't see land but I knew where it was. I knew we were almost there. 'lus, the airport was right on the coastline and so I wouldn't see it until we were ractically on top of it.

Please fasten your seatbelts" came a voice above my head. I clicked on my eatbelt. Mollie and Ava did the same.

This time, Grandad McCain had his seatbelt on very tightly indeed! He vasn't visiting the lavatory that landing - that was certain.

As the plane taxied around the airfield, I looked at the golden Australian sun hining down on the flat sunburnt Australian bush. The airport was in the niddle of nowhere right on the coast.

I couldn't see the sea. The airport buildings were in the way.

We'll ask to see it later" said Ava to me and Mollie. We agreed.

Our next step was to pick up Snowball and the baggage and get a taxi to the amping shop! Soon we'd be camping and would celebrate Uncle Jake's irthday - I'd bought him a compass with his name printed on the North pointer.

CHAPTER FOUR

THE SHOP INCIDENT

Soon we were off the plane and had collected Snowball.

"Woof!" she cried happily and she gave us all her best licks! The great thing about Snowball's licks are that they aren't very wet and it's very pleasant for her to lick you! (Not that I would mind a wet licky dog).

We had to wait a while because Grandad had gone to the toilet in the airport. By the time he came back to us he said he had also paid a visit to the gift shop and had bought a glass model of Sydney Opera House saying it was the airport we had just left, though it didn't look anything like it.

A taxi soon pulled up. It had been arranged to pick us up and take us to a small town. The driver was called Dave.

Dad and Jake opened the boot and started packing our things in. Everyone else found a seat. The taxi was a seven seater, so Dad and Jake sat on the roof! Snowball also insisted on sitting with the two on the roof - there'd be lots of wind up there and she liked wind!

"I'll just check the tyres" said Dave, "I'm sure I ran over a nail or something". He spoke with an Australian accent - I liked it!

He checked all the tyres but didn't find a puncture so we set off! The car rolled away and was soon on the outback roads of Australia!

I wished I was on the roof too. I would have had a great view. It was also very stuffy inside the taxi.

"Can we stop the car a minute?" said Ava.

Dave rolled the taxi to a stop and Ava got out. She took a picture of the view with her phone and then climbed onto the car roof.

"Coming Bobby?" she asked.

Not only I went onto that taxi's roof, but so did everyone else! We put a bathing towel down first because the roof was hot from the sun.

"I don't think you're supposed to do that" said Dave - he grinned, "but I don't wanna spoil your holiday so you're okay. No one's going to stop you out here anyway".

The taxi continued. We had a beautiful view and we saw a load of bounding kangaroos!

Soon the taxi reached a small town which Dave said was bound to have a camping shop.

We all said goodbye to Dave and stood on the pavement watching the taxi drive away. It beeped twice. I chuckled to myself. Snowball nuzzled Ava until she was paying attention, then she began licking herself. She then went to a shady spot and lay down, panting.

She was too hot. We too suddenly realised how hot it was.

Jake took out his little pocket thermometer and cried aloud, "It's over forty degrees!"

The sun was bright and so I tilted my beige cap down to shade my eyes. Julie did the same with her dark, blue cap.

Ava put her dirty blonde hair into a bun and Mollie put her auburn hair into two bunches.

Grandad wanted to take off his cowboy hat but didn't want to show his baldness, so he couldn't.

"I could do with an ice cream" said Dad. Grandad squealed.

"Oh, yes!" he cried, "I want an ice cream!"

So we started looking for an ice cream shop but first we found a camping shop and we decided to buy the important things first, much to Grandad's disgust.

The camping shop was a small one painted black. The paint was starting to peel too. It had one large window next to a door made of glass.

We went in, leaving Snowball tied to a lamppost outside. A friendly shopkeeper was sat behind a till reading a book.

There were shelves everywhere. They towered above the ground and were full of tents packed in boxes and bags. There were smaller shelves stood in the middle of the shop full of camping gear. Near the till was a clothes rack full of expensive camping clothes.

We started looking for our tents. I had to find one for Mum, Dad and I. Ava had to find one for herself, her mum and dad and Snowball. Mollie had to look for one for just herself and the same went for Grandad.

I found a dark green tunnel tent - one of those things with two or three bedrooms and a porch-way - that would do for my family.

Ava found a light-grey tunnel tent big enough for her family.

"Look, Snowball can sit in that porch-way" she said, looking at the picture on the tent packet.

"This one's big enough for me!" said Mollie, who had found a small blue tent, "I'll be able to carry it myself".

"I'LL HAVE THIS ONE!!!" shouted Grandad. I think he thought that when he shouted and yelled it made him sound excited - it only made him sound silly.

Grandad was pointing to a HUGE wigwam thing in a box as big as a small fridge lay on its back!

"You won't even be able to get it down from that top shelf - let alone out of this shop!" said Julie.

"Course I will" said Grandad and began pulling the huge box off the very top shelf.

Unfortunately, the box caught on a part of the shelf and Grandad couldn't move it - he pulled hard and the wigwam/tent thing came crashing to the ground along with the WHOLE shelf.

CHAPTER FIVE

GRANDAD ON FIRE

As the shelf and wigwam/tent box crashed down, Grandad tried to leap out of the way.

He was too late - the whole shelf crashed down on him, then the rack where the tents sat crashed into one of the small shelves in the middle of the shop.

Everybody burst into laughter - even the shopkeeper!

A bottle of methylated spirit burst all over Grandad from head to toe. This made him skid over the shop into yet another shelf. He must have hit a lighter box or something because he suddenly went up in hot flames! The methylated spirit made the flames spread quickly and Grandad now looked like a fire monster!

"Help!" screamed Grandad. He rushed outside in search of water - going outside an air conditioned shop and into forty degrees of sunlight in a hot country when you're alight with flames isn't a very good idea - Grandad's cowboy hat was immediately smouldered away leaving him with a new hairstyle made of orange flames. I thought it quite suited him!

The shopkeeper grabbed a fire extinguisher and darted after the smouldering Grandad, shooting the foam at him whenever he could.

Grandad (who couldn't see because of the flames) thought that the shopkeeper was a gangster shooting at him with a pistol. He was absolutely petrified!

I seriously cannot think what the Australian folk thought when they saw a blazing police officer (did I tell you he always wore his uniform, even on holiday?) rampaging through the town with a shopkeeper chasing him with a fire extinguisher.

By now, Grandad had done about three laps around the small town.

On the fourth lap he rushed passed us screaming “Help! Help!” We couldn’t elp the tears of laughter pouring down our cheeks. I heard a pedestrian say, He looks like he wants to be on fire the way he’s running from that xtinguisher!” Then I had to sit down!

Julie would have caught him but she couldn’t. Grandad didn’t show any igns of slowing. He was scared of the ‘gangster’ chasing him with a ‘gun’!

Finally, on Grandad’s fifth lap, I found another fire extinguisher and jumped ut into the middle of the road! I fired the foam just as Grandad tried to escape. 'he shopkeeper closed in on him from behind. The two of us managed to put ut Grandad’s fire and reassure him we weren’t gangsters!

The shopkeeper found Grandad a cloth to wipe away the foam and fetched im a glass of water.

We saw (when Grandad McCain had scrubbed the white foam away) that his lothes were burnt black and the bottom half of his pants had smouldered away. Ie now looked like he was wearing black shorts!

I don’t want that tent” Grandad decided.

Well at least you’ve made up your mind” said Mum.

Let’s go and choose another” said Julie.

I’m NOT going back into that shop” said Grandad, “I’ll just sleep outside on ne ground”.

Nine of the most poisonous snakes go hunting at night in Australia” said the hopkeeper who didn’t want to lose a customer.

Well in THAT case I’ll certainly buy a tent!” cried Grandad.

And with that he strode into the shop and bought, not one, but two tents - one ɔ put inside the other (to make it what he called ‘snake proof’).

Grandad also bought a set of expensive camping clothes and a new hat - a red cap to cover up his baldness.

“Don’t spend all your money at once” warned Julie.

“You really expect me to go around Australia for a fortnight wearing black crispy clothes that might, at any moment, disintegrate or something?” said Grandad.

“Now for an ice cream shop!” said Dad.

We untied Snowball whilst she went mad! (barking).

We didn’t manage to find an ice cream shop but found a cake shop that sold them!

As well as ice creams, everybody bought three small buns each!

I saw Grandad reading a small leaflet. I asked what it was about.

“It’s about camping. I don’t really understand it though” Grandad said. He showed me the title. It said;

‘Camping For Dummies’

“It sounds perfect for you” I said.

The buns were absolutely perfect - they had a base of something like sponge cake mixture and were topped with a caramel flavoured icing!

Suddenly a man appeared behind Grandad and started nudging him. He looked a bit older than Grandad and wore a pair of black reading glasses. He was bald and was wearing a light pink tourist’s jacket as well as some beige shorts.

“Excuse me” he was saying, “Excuse me, are you Mr McCain?”

“Yes!” said Grandad, turning around, “Who are you?”

“Do you have the same name as your surname?” asked the man.

“Yes, but who are YOU?” cried Grandad.

“What’s your middle name?” asked the man, not taking any notice of Grandad’s questions.

“Martin” answered Grandad, “But WHO are YOU?”

“Where do you live?” asked the man. Grandad seemed about to answer this but Julie stopped him.

“How do you know this man isn’t trying to steal your personal details?” she said, “Before we answer your questions, mister...” said Mum, turning to the mysterious man, “Tell us all who you are!”

“Don’t you know?” asked the man looking at Grandad questioningly. Grandad shook his head.

“It’s me, Thomas!” the man cried.

Grandad suddenly recognised the man and sprang up from his chair.

“Oh it’s YOU!” he shouted, pumping Thomas’s arm up and down, “I didn’t recognise you! You’ve changed! And what happened to your moustache? Have you lost it?”

Oh great, I thought, what’s going to happen now?

CHAPTER SIX

THOMAS AND HIS HELICOPTER

It was half past three by the time Thomas and my Grandad had finished talking and even then Jake had to butt in to warn them of the time.

"We'll have to set off looking for a taxi if we're going to get to our camping spot before dark. It's about 800 miles from here" Jake said.

"No worries" said Thomas standing up, "I'll fly you all over in less than twenty minutes!"

"What?" everyone cried.

"He has a helicopter! He has a helicopter!" cried Grandad, "He'll fly us there!"

"Does he really have a helicopter? asked Mollie.

"I have indeed" said Thomas, "she's called Betty - a real beauty!"

"What kind of helicopter is 'she'?" asked Dad.

"Robinson R44" said Thomas, "I sometimes call her Robin! She's pretty fast". Like Dave the taxi driver, Thomas spoke with an Australian accent!

"But Robinson R44s are tiny!" cried Jake, "Your helicopter won't fit us all".

"Trips!" cried Grandad, "I bet he'll take us in trips!"

"Course I will" said Thomas, "Now, twenty minutes to get there and back, there are nine altogether including the dog, so that's three trips".

After a pause, Thomas said "It'll take one hour at the most!"

"Much quicker than a taxi!" cried Grandad!

"You'd get there at midnight if you took one of those rotten taxis" said Thomas.

After a long discussion about this proposal we all accepted and allowed Thomas to lead us to his helicopter.

Then for the first time he realised that Snowball was actually our dog. The shop had allowed dogs. There was a sign outside saying;

'DOGS ARE WELCOME. NO MISBEHAVING ADULTS'

Snowball had wandered around the shop so often that Thomas didn't know who the owners were, but when he found out he was mightily impressed, "Beautiful dogs huskies are - always wanted one! They're not a bit like those ugly mongrels some people own".

"Mongrels are NOT ugly!" cried Ava and I. Ava continued, "I haven't met a human yet who looks nearly as nice as a big (or small) mongrel!"

There wasn't a single animal that Ava, Mollie or I disliked - from the tiny bluebottle flies to elephants, and slimy slugs to scaly snakes, and flat flatfish (or olive flounders) to tall giraffes, all were loved! I call worms 'Miniature English Snakes'!

"Who exactly is Thomas?" Julie asked Grandad as Thomas walked us down a street.

"Thomas Buckle is my childhood friend" said Grandad, "We used to go to the same school. We became best friends".

"Yes, until you jumped off the school diving board onto me instead of the water" said Thomas.

"Well, I didn't know at the time" said Grandad going red.

"When I grew up" said Thomas, "I moved from England to Australia - I'll tell you all something, it's miles better".

"You've caught the accent strongly" said Dad, admiringly.

“I’ve lived here ever since” Thomas went on, “I’m usually down in Sydney but I came up here to visit a nephew”.

We rounded an alleyway between two posh houses and there in front of us was parked a small, red painted Robinson R44. The cockpit, or whatever you call it, was mostly glass and there were about five comfortable seats inside! It looked very cute and small.

On one side of the helicopter was painted in black letters the words ‘Quick-Betty’.

“Now” said Thomas, “Who’s going on the first flight?”

“I’ll go” said Dad, “We’ll take the tents and things”.

“I’ll go” said Mum, “I can start putting up the tents then”.

“I wanna come” moaned Grandad.

“Me and Jake’ll stay and watch the children” said Julie.

“They can go on the second trip or flight” said Jake, “Julie and I will go on the third flight”.

We began packing our things into the helicopter’s storage compartment - everything fit except my family’s dark green tunnel tent which was too big.

“Take it on our flight” I said.

“Yes, well do that” said Thomas. He climbed into the helicopter and my mum and dad and Grandad McCain followed.

The glass of the helicopter was a kind that you cannot see in but you can see out, so I couldn’t see what the passengers inside were doing but I guessed they were putting on some headphones.

The engines started and the propellers whizzed around! We watchers had to run for shelter when the dust was blown into our eyes!

Betty the helicopter rose into the sky. I waved and a light was flashed in eturn. The helicopter flew away fast and was lost behind a white, fluffy cloud.

Amazing, isn't it?" said Julie to us, "A minute ago we were worrying about inding a taxi - now we're waiting for a helicopter to pick us up which is piloted y my dad's school friend!"

Absolutely amazing!" said Mollie grinning, "This is very exciting" I said, "Yes it was going to be very exciting indeed!"

CHAPTER SEVEN

FLYING

After about twenty minutes the little helicopter was back, though this time it was empty except for Thomas. He opened the door and called in his Australian accent, “Come on kids”.

Ava, Mollie and I clambered into the tiny flying machine and found our seats. I was sat in the back row of three on the left side with Snowball in the middle. Ava was on the other side of her to the right. Mollie was sat next to Thomas in the front.

Julie was around the right side of the helicopter packing my big tunnel tent into the baggage area.

After shutting all the doors, Thomas leaned over to us all and whispered in a very secret Australian whisper, “Can you keep a secret?”

“Sure - what is it?” asked Mollie. Thomas revealed three tiny glass bottles containing white powder.

“This” said Thomas, “is luck-powder. Eat just one little jar of it and you will not have any accidents that day - extremely useful when flying because you know you won’t crash”.

We all took the jars of ‘luck-powder’ and ate it all. I didn’t believe in good fortune and luck and all the rest. I knew that the white powder was sugar, but still, who can turn down a bottle of sweet sugar? Not me!”

“Right!” said Julie, appearing at the window, “All’s ready for take-off out here!” She backed up and stood with Jake. They were stood way out-of-the-way of the helipad so that dust wouldn’t get them.

Thomas passed us each a set of headphones.

"It gets loud in here when the propellers start" he said. Mollie and I put on ours.

Ava managed to securely strap a pair of headphones to Snowball's head then she put hers on her own head!

The engine was then turned on and the propellers started spinning! Then suddenly - WHOOSH! Betty lifted her under-racking off the ground and rose high!

I saw Julie and Jake waving up to us. I asked Thomas if he would flash to her.

"Don't be silly" Thomas said, "This helicopter doesn't flash or anything".

"Oh, so you didn't flash us when we waved earlier?" I said.

"No, the helicopter just flashes when she feels like it!" replied Thomas.

The helicopter flew over streams, rivers and sometimes kangaroos!

"I want to show you guys something, if you want me to" said Thomas.

"What is it?" asked Ava.

"Whales!" cried Thomas, "It's a secret spot I know that's great for spotting whales. They're there all the time. It's a little bit out of the way though..." he paused and gave three hard coughs - he didn't sound too well, "...so if you don't want to we won't go there" he said.

"Of course we'd go there" cried Ava, "We love animals".

Thomas swung the helicopter violently right. We saw the coast coming up, containing the beautiful greeny-blue waters!

At intervals, Thomas (who looked over 60) kept giving huge coughs. I put it down to old age.

After six minutes we couldn't see the land behind us.

"They should be somewhere round here. Keep an eye out" said Thomas.

We all scanned the ocean but couldn't see a single whale.

COUGH-COUGH!!

Thomas had started coughing again, then suddenly Thomas's arms went limp and he closed his eyes. I was the only one who saw this. The others (including Snowball) were on a whale-hunt.

"What kind of whales are they?" asked Mollie, who had her back to the unconscious Thomas, "I'm waiting", she said impatiently. She swung round to see why Thomas wasn't answering. When she saw that he had fainted she let out a scream!

"What?" cried Ava, "What kind of whale have you seen?" She thought Mollie had seen a whale.

Suddenly Thomas's body fell limply forward and pushed the control stick. The whole helicopter dipped with its 'nose' pointing to the ocean!

Ava shot round and yelped. So did Snowball!

I took off my straps holding me to my seat and leaned into the front. I lunged Thomas's body onto Mollie's lap and sat in his place. The whole time the helicopter was racing towards the sea!

I grabbed the main control stick and yanked it right back. The helicopter was forced to pull up very suddenly and it stalled. We went crashing through the waves until fully submerged. We then bobbed back up to the surface. The helicopter - you see - had safety floats on the racks on the underside! These allowed us to sit there and bob!

Water had filled the engine so the propellers couldn't work until the engine was emptied. We saw that the water was dripping out so I said, "We'll just have to wait here until all the water's drained out, then I'll try and fly us back to land". So we waited.

CHAPTER EIGHT

THE WHALES

"I wonder what the grown ups will think when we don't show up" said Ava.

"We left Jake and Julie all by themselves at that little town" I said.

"Let's search the helicopter" said Mollie, "I'll go and search the storage compartment outside".

"What about the water?" I asked.

"There's a little white racking that acts as a step for getting in" said Mollie, "I'll use that".

Out she went. When she stepped onto the racking/steps the whole helicopter rocked about!

"I don't really call this a holiday, do you?" said Ava, looking under her chair.

"No" I said, "I call it an adventure. A good proper adventure! But I do understand the possibility of death - and I'm fully aware of it!"

"Hey, what's this?" cried Ava, pulling a tin box out from under her chair. On it was printed the words;

Emergency Box

"Open it!" I cried. Ava took off the lid. Inside there was the following;

Three red torches called flares,

Two white spotlights,

A plaster kit,

A wrap of bandages,

A tub of matches,

Two kits of fire lighters,

and five red things wrapped up into something like a backpack.

“They’re parachutes!” I cried, “but they do not come in useful with the situation we’re in now sadly”.

“Hey Mollie!” shouted Ava, “Come and see what we’ve found”.

Mollie came quickly in - rocking the helicopter side-to-side. Snowball whimpered.

“Look, we’ve found an Emergency Box!” I said, “Though nothing in it is helpful to us”.

“What about the spotlight and flares?” asked Mollie, “Couldn’t we use them to signal to land?”

“We could” said Ava, “Though we’d have to wait till dark because otherwise the lights wouldn’t show”.

“I think it would be quicker waiting for the engine to drain all the water” I said, “Then all I have to do is fly us back to land”.

“We’ll try whichever comes first” said Mollie, “If the engine drains its water first then we’ll give a shot at flying the helicopter home - and if darkness is first we’ll shine our flares!”

“Did you find anything outside?” asked Ava.

“Not yet,” said Mollie, “but I could see something red. I was going to grab it but you called me in”.

Go and find out what it was" I said, "We'll have another look underneath these eats". And off Mollie went, back onto the white racking. Once again the elicopter wobbled as she sat on the water.

Whoops - almost dropped it" came Mollie's voice, "Well you two, it's a fire xtinguisher...what is THAT?"

Ava and I waited for Mollie to speak again, expecting her to have found omething else in the storage area. She called again, "Bobby, Ava, quick - come nd see".

We both rushed out onto the racking. This made the helicopter tilt over most errribly. What we saw now was the plain blue ocean stretching as far as the orizon. There was one seagull that was visible. It was flying low looking for sh!

What was it?" said Ava, turning to Mollie to see if she had found anything om the compartment. She was holding the fire extinguisher in one hand and aid, "I...I think I saw a whale!"

A whale? What kind?" asked Ava.

I only saw the fin" said Mollie, "it was black".

Just then, a huge orca whale heaved itself out of the sea and grabbed the low-ying seagull by its tail. The poor bird tried to escape but the orcas pulled it raight into the cold water. The whale disappeared after splashing gracefully ith her tail!

Whew!" I cried, "What a sight!"

Suddenly Snowball fell into the water. She had come treading on the racking nd had slipped in!

At the same time the fin of the giant orca whale came into sight - it was eading straight for us!

Ava took a leap and splashed into the sea. She grabbed Snowball and hurled er into the helicopter. I helped Ava up yelling, "Mollie - Mollie quick get nside!"

Orca whales - in case you didn't know - have been known to attack (and kill seals. Most of the time they don't even eat their prey, they just kill for the fun o it. They sometimes get their targets over their tails and flip them over and over until death occurs!

This is exactly why these whales have been given the nickname 'killer-whales'!

We all huddled back into the helicopter and shut the door!

"Watch out - here she comes!" I cried, looking through the glass at the fun coming closer and closer - then WHAM!

The great creature hit our helicopter making it rock dangerously!

WHAM! The orca gave our machine a flick with her tail!

"She definitely knows we're in here!" cried Ava - WHAM! She bumped us from underneath!

I quickly got into the driving seat and switched on the engine - WHAM! WHAM! The orca was getting bold now and was hitting us rapidly! WHAM - WHAM! Two more!

I pressed a button that made the propellers start whizzing!

There came a crunching noise as the great whale ripped off the landing rack - thankfully not touching the floats. WHAM - WHAM - WHAM!

"She's hitting us with the racking!" cried Ava. She gave a scream. The orca hac jumped out of the water again - this time in front of us - with the top of her hea facing us!

With a roar she let out a gush of water, out of that little hole-thingy that mos whales have. The water racked against our windshield and made us all jump!

She then hit against our helicopter again. In doing this the whale could easil sink us. I had to bring the machine into the air before it was too late.

“Look over there!” shouted Ava. Mollie, Snowball and I looked and saw that the large orca whale wasn’t alone any longer. Five or six more whale-fins were now visible - all heading towards us. They all began ‘whamming’ us as hard as they could! WHAM...WHAM! The underside of our helicopter was now very dented and bumped. One of the floats had snapped off - this meant that Betty tilted over to one side!

Half of my window was submerged in water. I could clearly see at least fourteen big orca whales all swimming around us, trying to break us out!

If I was going to get us out of there alive, the time was now! If the other float was bitten off we would sink to the bottom of the ocean!

WHAM! A large orca jumped at us - hitting the side!

I pulled up with one of my control sticks. The propellers struggled. The engine (because we were tilting so much) kept taking in seeps of water. The water made the engine keep stalling!

At last the heavy little helicopter - dented as she was - lifted herself out of the waves into the air, but before I could pull any higher, a HUGE orca whale (obviously the head of the group) leaped clean out of the water and snatched hold of our tail wing! The orca pulled us straight back into the sea!

Our tail rudder was completely ripped off and was dropped to the sea-bed!

I piloted our helicopter into the air again but this time much higher out of reach of the orca whales.

“Whew!” sighed Ava, “We’re safe!”

But she was wrong!

CHAPTER NINE

MAYDAY

"Hey, what's that in the distance?" suddenly said Mollie, pointing through the helicopter windshield.

I had managed quite well in piloting the flimsy thing high enough so that the large orca whales couldn't reach us - though they still tried jumping at us!

We were now looking at what Mollie was pointing at - a patch of land! Right on the horizon was a small strip of sand from a beach of some land!

"It's Australia!" cried Ava, "We must have drifted closer inland when we were left bobbing all that time!"

"It looks a lot greener!" I said as I moved the helicopter closer, "I wonder which part we're at".

"Speed up!" said Mollie.

I pushed my control stick forwards and our little machine rushed ahead!

"The sand looks much whiter here" I said "Are you sure it is Australia?"

"Yes - of course it is" said Ava, "Why shouldn't it be? It...it...it does look a bit funny doesn't it?"

"Check the radar" said Mollie. I checked and saw that we were facing a land called;

AUST

"Yep!" I said, "It is Australia. Those letters mean AUSTralia!"

I swerved a bit but nothing happened on the radar! I swerved again but the picture on the radar was just the same! I swerved again. It was clear that the radar was broken.

"Hey, stop jerking!" said Mollie, "Thomas's body keeps almost slipping off me!"

We were almost on top of what we thought was Australia - we couldn't see the other side of course but found out afterwards that it was a small island in the shape of a kidney bean!

Suddenly all the control screens switched off! The engine also went blank!

I had to think fast. The helicopter dropped out of the sky and began racing to Australia!

"It isn't Australia!" cried Mollie suddenly. She began to quail!

I also saw that the island wasn't Australia. It was just a bean shaped flat island with white beaches and thick forests!

I tried desperately to steer Betty towards the sea but the orca whales had bitten off our steering equipment!

"Grab the parachutes!" I shouted making a quandary!

Ava opened the tin labelled 'Emergency Box' and took out three red parachutes!

We each strapped one to our backs. They fastened like an ordinary rucksack! I slid open the helicopter door and gasped as the wind rushed at me!

The drop was horrifying! It must have been at least eight hundred feet high!

Mollie closed her eyes and sort of stepped out into the air!

I watched her plummet to the island! Ava grabbed hold of the whimpering Snowball, took a good grip and leaped out of our helicopter!

I didn't jump - something held me back and I couldn't move.

I couldn't blame myself for being rooted to the spot. Standing at the open door of an out-of-control helicopter with the pilot lying next to me, totally unconscious, is quite an aura of panic!

At that moment, a seagull sadly lunged into the engine of the helicopter, which at once exploded and a trail of black smoke spewed behind me!

This explosion gave me some courage and I took a deep breath, closed my eyes and leaped fully out of the crashing helicopter into the air!

I stayed where I was for around half a second and then I dived!

At that moment, every single bone in my entire body rushed to my back, trying their hardest to break through my clothes! My insides also darted back and tried to escape but I thankfully hadn't eaten anything except the vegan nug-mugs on the plane and the ice creams and buns from the cake shop.

I wondered whether my parachute would work properly, but found it better not to wonder these things!

As I fell, I could see Mollie and Ava both plummeting to earth. I saw Ava (who was carrying Snowball close to her chest) struggling around frantically. I tucked in my limbs so that I dropped down to her. When I reached her I spread out my arms and legs and I slowed my descent at once.

"What's the matter?" I shouted.

"I can't pull my parachute string!" shouted back Ava, "If I do I'll drop snowball!

I sort of swam over to her, grabbed her and pulled my own string. My parachute immediately broke open and unfolded!

We both began drifting slowly to the ground! Mollie (who hadn't activated her parachute) whizzed passed us, enjoying this skydiving experience!

"We're going to crash!" shouted Ava, "I know we are!"

CHAPTER TEN

NO MAN HAS SET FOOT HERE BEFORE

.s we flitted down to the island we saw Mollie activate her parachute and begin itting as we were doing.

Unfortunately, my parachute had a big hole in it which made it difficult to :eer!

Above us, the helicopter whizzed down to the island. It landed in the distance nd exploded, probably killing the unconscious Thomas who was still aboard it!

I tried steering my parachute into the shallow part of the ocean around the .land, but - as I said before - the hole in the parachute made steering almost npossible and we ended up cruising over the treetops so low that if I hadn't fted my legs up they would have knocked against them!

Ava suddenly lost her grip of Snowball and she plummeted to the ground - ıe hit a flat black rock and immediately fell silent! We had been about fifteen :et in the air when she had dropped!

Ava struggled to free herself from me so she could see to Snowball, but I held er. I wasn't going to let her drop as well as Snowball.

I held on to Ava firmly until finally she reached her head down and bit my rm hard! I then let go and fortunately Ava fell into a pile of soft sand! She olled over but stood up unharmed.

I tried landing my parachute but smashed into a pine tree!

The strings of the parachute got tangled into the leaves of the trees around me nd I was left suspended about eight feet from the ground - which is quite high hen you come to think about it!

In the end Mollie (who had landed her parachute successfully) had to come and help me down, then we both went to find our two companions.

We found them with success quite near my crashed parachute, which had been left behind. Ava had carried Snowball to a shady spot. You must remember that even though we weren't in Australia, the weather was still the same - 40 degrees!

Mollie fetched some seawater in her hands and poured it - or what was left o it - onto the head of the unconscious Snowball.

After ten minutes Snowball was herself again, bounding around as usual!

We found a beach that would be a nice place to bed down for the night (as i was already getting dark). You can see now how quick at making plans we are. Ava collected some grass and lay it down on the sand as a bed. Mollie (who wa quite knowledgeable on rocks) went looking for some kind of stone to create fire and I helped collect the bedding with Ava.

"I wonder where we are" said Ava, "We're certainly not in Australia because I caught a glimpse of the other sides of this island when we were in the helicopter".

"It looks like we're the only ones on this island" I said, "No man has ever set foot here! And that's quite something!"

"It certainly is" said Ava, "Ah - here's Mollie. Did you find anything? Your pockets are bulging".

"They're full of quartz" she said. I groaned.

"Don't tell me we're going to have to store all your beloved stones whilst we'r here?" I cried.

"Well, this one's special anyhow" Mollie said, taking a black rock out of her pocket. It gleamed and shined in the evening sun.

"It's flint!" she said triumphantly, "Rub it against some steel and it'll create fire!"

"Great!" Ava and I cried, "Let's build a campfire!"

So we made a campfire like my dad had taught us all - using rocks to make a wall around the fire pit and filling the pit with twigs, leaves and practically anything made of wood.

"Where's some steel?" I asked. We all paused and looked at each other, groaning.

Mollie gave a cry, "We can use Snowball's collar, medal thingy! It's made of stainless STEEL!"

I took off Snowball's collar and swiped the steel medal/name tag across the piece of flint! A bright spark dropped onto the ready-made fire pit and it smouldered a bit before turning to a bright orange flame that rapidly burned away the dry wood!

I was so astonished at how easy the whole procedure had been, I dropped the collar into the flames by accident!

"Quick, get a stick!" cried Ava, "We can fish it out".

But by the time we had found a suitable stick, Snowball's collar was just a crispy black wire! Ava tried fishing it out and she was forced to throw it into the roaring fire!

It was now moonlight! The fire flowed and cracked, making weird shadows that danced and wobbled!

There wasn't a single cloud in the sky! We could all see the white dazzling stars as we sat around our fire.

"What should we do?" I said, "How do we get help?"

"Should we just wait?" suggested Mollie.

"No" said Ava firmly, "We'd have to start hunting around for some kind of fruit - I'm certainly not eating any animals we find".

“Yes” I said, “Once we get settled here with provisions and an abode we can then start thinking about help”.

“Right” said Mollie, “Tomorrow’s plans are to find food and make a home, right?”

“That’s right” Ava said, “Let’s bed down - I’m tired”.

We all bedded down on our heaps of long grass.

“What a beautiful green island this is” said Mollie.

“It’s our island!” I replied, “It’s our own island”.

CHAPTER ELEVEN

OUR ISLAND

I woke with the sun blazing into my eyes and the sand burning my back!

I stood up shaking the sand off my clothes. Snowball awoke and shook herself - she had slept next to Ava all night!

I got quite a shock when I saw something large and brown moving towards the sea - it was a gorgeous brown deer!

The beach we had slept on was the shape of the letter 'C'. The forest of palm trees came up the bottom left corner of the 'C' shaped beach. There was also a small, thin beach of white sand on the other side of the forest. We had slept on the sand nearest to the forest where we had found the softest patch of sand!

I stocked up our fire pit (which had gone out in the middle of the night when we were all asleep) with more wood I found scattered about. I didn't light it. I was waiting for the girls first. Anyway, I thought, who wants a warm fire on this hot day?

Mollie woke first, having dreamt that she was chasing Thomas (who was now dead) around an island known as 'Our island'.

She piled her many quartz stones next to her 'bed'.

"Now, what kind of a home should we have?" asked Mollie, "A treehouse? Like the Swiss Family Robinson? A little hut? Or something else?"

"We'll discuss our home when we're all awake" I said, "If you're bored you can hunt for food".

And so Mollie set off to look for some food.

“No meat!” I called after her. She nodded and disappeared behind a clump of trees.

The first thing I did was to wash. I undressed and dived into the cold ocean, but it wasn’t as cold as I had imagined - the water had been heated up by the sun!

“Like a huge jacuzzi!” I said to myself.

When I had finished my bathe, I came back up to Ava and Snowball. Ava was now awake and was busily being licked by Snowball.

“Morning” I said.

“It’s beautiful!” Ava cried, “Look, what’s that?”

I looked to where she was pointing and rising from the horizon was a column of black smoke!

“From the helicopter crash, I expect” I said.

“Where’s Mollie?” asked Ava, noticing for the first time that Mollie wasn’t around.

“She’s gone hunting for food” I said, “Snowball, that’s enough barking”.

“Should we go food hunting, then?” Ava asked.

“Yes” I said, “We’ll meet again at this bridge. Let’s split up. I’ll go that way, and you go that way”.

“Right” said Ava, “Come on Snowball. Bye, Bobby”.

“Seeya” I said, mimicking the Australian accent.

We set out and found a way that went into thick vegetation. I had travelled for about ten minutes before spotting a small fruit growing on a bush. I bent down to investigate. The fruit was about the size of a cherry (maybe a bit bigger), perfectly round. It was smooth and shiny like a cherry and was the pinky-orange colour of a ripe peach.

I soon noticed that, hidden underneath the leaves there were thousands more f these cherry sized, peach looking berries! They definitely weren't bird-erries, that was sure!

Just as I was cautiously about to test my berry, the leaves of a fern bush next me parted and a young female deer came striding over to the berry bush! She idn't show any signs of fear! I suppose, I thought, I suppose it's because no uman has ever been here. She hasn't learned to fear mankind yet!

I reached out and gingerly stroked the young doe's back. It was surprisingly oft and velvety! The beautiful creature didn't even twitch when I touched her!

The doe bent down and began munching away at the berries, taking a lot of are not to eat the leaves.

Seeing the deer eating these suspicious berries gave me confidence, although n no account was I going to test a berry on an animal, seeing the deer casually ating the fruit showed that they were not poisonous - unless these deer had a uper-detoxicating gut.

I immediately tried my single berry which I had been holding as I watched e deer. It tasted WONDERFUL!

The berry tasted like apple mixed in a mixer along with a dollop of white ees' honey. After I had eaten all of my single berry I waited to see if any bad de effects occurred and after waiting eight minutes I decided that this fruit was armless. I picked a HUGE bunch (which is quite difficult when you've got a eer standing next to you trying to gobble up all the berries at the same time) to ke back to our beach.

I ended up picking so many pinky-orange berries that I had to store some in y hat turned upside down and some in my pockets.

I then left the berry bush and the female deer and tried to find our beach. I oon found it and I also found Mollie there.

I guessed you'd gone food hunting" she said.

Did you find anything?" I asked.

“Nope, did you?”

“I did indeed” I said. I piled all the berries onto a big palm leaf and showed them to Mollie - she was impressed.

“How do we know they’re not poisonous?” she said, “We need some kind of proof - but we can’t test it on an animal and...”

“Mollie” I said holding her shoulder, “You’re talking to the proof”.

“What do you mean?” she asked.

“I’ve eaten some and do I look poisoned?” I replied.

I told her about the deer and how I had seen her eating the berries so I tried one.

Mollie picked up one of the berries and popped it into her mouth. At the fir chew she exclaimed, “Oh, it’s perfect, it’s better than any fruit I’ve tasted!”

Ava suddenly appeared at our beach and called us, waving something like a oval shaped stone above her head.

“Look what I’ve found!” she cried, “It’s a pineapple!”

CHAPTER TWELVE

JAKE'S BIRTHDAY

That night we all shared out the pineapple and a few berries! We cut the pineapple using a sharp piece of wood that we found.

After our meal we went to our piles of grass and sand which we called 'beds' and dozed off at once.

Next morning we all (including Snowball) woke at the same time. We knew exactly what special day it was.

"Happy birthday, Dad - wherever you are" said Ava.

"Happy birthday, Uncle Jake" I said, staring over the horizon at the sea.

"Happy birthday, bro" said Mollie.

That day before doing any jobs, the three of us - no four, counting in Snowball - made a 'happy birthday' sign out of rocks on the beach. It said;

HAPPY 27th BIRTHDAY JAKE

"Now, what should we do?" asked Ava.

"Well, our plans were to build a shelter - or house!" I said.

"But what kind and how?" said Mollie.

"We'll build a hut" I said, walking over to our stock of firewood. I chose a tall, strong, pole-like stick and carried it to a pile of soft grass and drove it into the ground.

"In placing the first brick of our home, I announce I am captain of the building work" I cried. The others laughed.

“Alright” said Mollie, “What are our orders, Captain Bobby?”

“Find more tall strong sticks like this one” I said pointing to the stick I had just hurled into the grass, “Get a stone each and hammer the sticks into the ground if they won’t go by body strength”.

My little ‘crew’ set to work building an abode for us. I helped them of course. I wouldn’t leave them both to do all the hard work themselves!

At last we had four strong wooden poles at the corners of our future house. It looked as though it was going to be a large four-poster-bed!

“Next we need some kind of rope” I said, thinking of all the exotic kinds of rope, “Vines, has anyone seen any vines?”

“I’ve got string” said Mollie, “I always carry a ball of string around, though I don’t know why”.

“Great!” I said, “Pass it here”. She passed and I took it. I looked around, “We’ll now need a really long pole that will reach from each of these poles we’ve dug into the ground”.

We all set about looking for some REALLY LONG and STRONG poles of wood.

In the end it was Snowball who found us the perfect stick.

“Now we need one more, just the same as this one” I said, “Good girl, Snowball”.

“Woof!” thanked Snowball.

“What’s that?” suddenly said Ava. We looked and saw three deer!

“There’s a lot of deer here” I said, “In a way that’s a very good thing because it means there isn’t a predator here that kills them, so we don’t need to worry about leopards or jaguars or even tigers!”

"You say there's no predator here?" said Mollie who was hunting for wood, "Look at this! I thought it was a piece of wood!"

Ava and I ran over to her. We saw on the ground a bloodstained deer leg!

It had evidently been bitten off because there were teeth marks indented into the skin!

"So there is a predator about!" I cried, "we must watch out for him from now on!"

Believe it or not, Snowball is a vegetarian dog! Living off fruit and practically anything we children ate! Because of this, Snowball didn't touch the deer leg. She knew exactly what she was and wasn't allowed to eat!

When we returned to our building site we continued with our house. We kept making trips around the island when we couldn't find a suitable stick.

Soon we had finished the framework of the ground floor and began making the roof!

We managed to make a doorway, but no windows. At the end we stood back to take a look at our hard work.

"It rather looks like a skeleton!" remarked Mollie, "What do we fill all the gaps with?"

"With our parachutes!" I said, "We'll cover the whole thing over with the three parachutes! Obviously leaving a gap for the door!"

Ava and I went and fetched the parachutes, which were left exactly as we had left them, all tangled in a tree!

When we brought the parachutes back to our house, Mollie was roasting some berries over the fire.

"Hey, you two! Taste these!" she cried, "Put down those parachutes and come and have supper".

We both went over and tried a berry. They had a hard crust from the fire, which had burst a bit showing the light green blob of sweet jelly stuff!

"Oh, they're even better cooked!" I cried. The hard crispy crust (which had turned from pinky-orange to reddy-brown) tasted like apple skin but hotter, thicker and crispier, and the blob of light green jelly tasted exactly like hot pear and syrup!

"How simply divine!" Ava remarked.

"What made you cook them?" I asked.

"Well" said Mollie, "You left Snowball with me as you know and I lit the fire when I saw the sun going down. Snowball found our stock of berries and grabbed a mouthful and as she walked by the fire some fell out into the flames!"

"Go on" said Ava.

"Some berries were burnt right up but others (that fell out of the fire) were just nearly cooked. When I saw Snowball try one I tried one and when I found out how gorgeous they were I started cooking loads!"

Mollie paused after her rather long speech and popped a few cooked berries into her mouth!

"They're filling too!" said Ava surprised, "I'm full already. Bobby, let's go to bed now. We can finish the house tomorrow".

"Alright" I said, "I'm sleepy too. Night everyone".

We snuggled down into our grassy beds and dozed off! What a wonderful birthday Jake had - except that he wasn't there!

CHAPTER THIRTEEN

THE POISONOUS DART FROG

was now the third day on the island! We woke quite late that day and we uickly set to work building our home. We carried a single heavy red parachute d tied it to one half of the frame made of wood. We then brought another for e other half and did the same. We then lifted the remaining parachute onto the of! After making sure everything was properly tied down and was very cure, we began filling the inside floor with grass. We found some HUGE lm leaves and lay them down for our new beds!

I slid open parts of the parachutes to let light in. The sunlight also came rtly through too, in the same way any light does if you hold your fingers close the light kind of glows through! Now our house was filled with an orangey-red ow making it very cosy!

t needs a name" Mollie said, "We can't have a beautiful little house on a vely island without a name".

Let's call it 'Deer Cottage' because lots of deer always come visiting this each" Ava said, so Deer Cottage it was and once that day, a small male deer ent wandering in.

He thinks it's his cottage" I said, "Because of the name we gave it!"

We all went out food hunting. We had almost run out of berries and were oping to find another pineapple.

We all split up. I found a clear path and decided to follow it. It was definitely path made by the deer because I could sometimes spot a hoof print in the dry ud.

Very soon I found another berry bush infested with millions of berries! They ere all round, shiny, pinky-yellow and the size of a cherry! I filled my pockets nd my hat with the delicious fruit and then set off again.

Suddenly as I passed a dark green bush I saw a glint of yellow underneath i
I thought it was another set of berries so I bent down and checked under the bush. I saw a yellow frog, about as tall as a drawing pin. I knew instantly what species it was. It was a Poisonous Dart Frog! I mentioned it quite a while back in case you'd forgotten, the sweat of these tiny creatures is the most dangerous poison in the world. People of the ancient time used to hold these frogs over a fire to collect the poison and tip their arrows for their bows!

As I looked at the tiny frog he looked back at me out of jet black eyes like two marbles!

I backed out in retreat but the frog (who must have liked the look of me) darted onto my belly!

I froze. If - told myself - this little animal touches me, I'll die. I must get it off.

I slowly moved over to a tree and snapped off a stick. I gently helped the frog onto the stick and began the short journey to the ground.

But unfortunately, the Dart Frog quickly darted onto the collar of my jumper! I froze again! The dart frog was far too close to my skin now!

Quickly I got my stick and for the second time I helped the tiny animal onto it. I then threw the stick into the dark green bushes and ran for my life!

Something caught my eye as I was running - an oval shaped rock lying on the floor with little spiky leaves sprouting out of the top. It was a kind of greeny-yellow. At once I cried, "A pineapple!"

I stopped running and grabbed the fruit. I ran again - this time all the way back to our beach and house. Ava was there, looking pleased.

"Look what I've got" I said. I showed her the pineapple and she was overjoyed

"Look what I found" she said. I waited for her to show me some food but she took me into the house and pointed to the ceiling. I saw, dangling from a string four large coconuts!

“They’re full of juice!” Ava said, “I thought it would look nice if our food was hanging over us. Don’t they look fashionable?”

“They certainly do!” I cried, “Suppose one of them leaks in the night. The drips will drop straight into our mouths!”

“Perfect!” Ava said.

“Lets cook some of these berries, have half of the pineapple and a full coconut for tea!” I suggested.

“We’ll wait for Mollie first” Ava replied.

So we waited. We waited for an hour and a half and finally, Ava, Snowball and I had our food without her.

The food was delicious - especially the coconut milk - as I had had nothing to drink since we had arrived at the island! The berries had been roasted and were eaten quickly and the half-of-the pineapple was shared into two. We saved Mollie some but after another hour we ate it ourselves.

“Where is she?” said Ava at a quarter-to-nine.

“Let’s go hunting for her” I said, so we got up and walked off.

“Snowball should find her” said Ava, “Snowball, go find Mollie - find Mollie, where’s Mollie? Snowball, Mollie, go find!”

Snowball understood. With her nose to the ground she began wandering around the palm forest.

As we suddenly rounded a large rock, Snowball ran ahead. At once a volley of angry and distressed barks was heard!

Ava and I rushed on worriedly! Was Snowball being attacked?

As we ran to Snowball’s aid we heard a voice, “Snowball, get off my leg - I thought you were a predator!”

“It’s Mollie!” I cried. We rounded a bend and there was Mollie, lying on a pile of wood chippings.

“Sorry I’m so late” she said.

“What do you mean?” I said, “You’re not late. You haven’t even arrived back yet!”

“I was following a family of deer” Mollie said.

“Let’s get back” said Ava, “I’m tired”.

It was very dark and we almost got lost, but we thankfully found our home.

We fell asleep at once and had wonderful dreams!

CHAPTER FOURTEEN

THE HELICOPTER WRECK

Up until now we all hadn't taken any notice of the huge column of black smoke rising from the site of the helicopter crash. Today, the smoke was beginning to disappear!

So that day, after breakfast, we decided to trek over to the wreck and explore it.

"We may find that emergency box!" said Ava, "With those spotlights inside!"

We set off, taking some berries in our pockets for snacks.

The pillar of smoke (now quite thin) was our main guide. We could always look up and see the smoke and find the best route available!

Once or twice we found the carcass of a dead deer, but more often we found alive ones!

"The helicopter seems close now!" I said. I could see the pillar of smoke quite close to us. At any moment we would round a corner and there would be a frizzled up framework of a helicopter, possibly containing a crispy, burnt skeleton of Thomas!

Finally, we found the helicopter, which Thomas had named Betty! She had come crashing down and hit a rock then she must have skidded into place! She was brown and black everywhere. Little orange flames flickered here and there, but the black smoke still billowed out of the engine.

The windscreen had shattered out and some iron plating had popped off! She was a poor sight.

Of course - as we know - the rear wing was not there. It had been bitten off by the fierce orca whales!

We ran forward, avoiding the deadly looking smoke, and explored the wrecked Betty.

"Look at this!" shouted Mollie. When I looked and saw what she had found, an electric shock went down my spine, for sat on one of the helicopter seats was the bloodstained, black, frizzled skeleton of Thomas!

We left the skeleton after a while and continued looking around the helicopter.

"Here's the emergency box!" shouted Ava, "It's still got its items inside. I can feel them when I lift the box!"

"Open it, quick!" I said. Mollie and I were crowding round her with Snowball at our feet!

Ava opened the box! All the items were not harmed. One of the two spotlights was broken but other than that, nothing was burnt!

"And look at this!" cried Mollie from one side of the helicopter, "It's Bobby's tent!"

We saw that Mollie was holding the bag containing the dark-green tent that was supposed to have been for my family.

"We can use it in emergencies" I said.

"It ought to be in the emergency box" said Ava.

"Here, Mollie" I said, "Give the tent to me to carry".

Mollie handed me the tent. It had a black strap on the package which I slung over my shoulder.

"We'll take the emergency box too" said Ava, "I'll carry it".

We sat down for lunch at one o'clock (I could tell the time using my watch).

After our lunch - which was berries - we spent a further ten minutes xploring the helicopter wreck and then set off home!

We saw lots of deer. We soon discovered the island was full of them, which as lovely, and because no humans ever frightened them, they were extremely me!

After ages, Mollie exclaimed, "There's the sea, already!" We ran ahead but stead of the sea, we came running up to the shore of a small pond! Behind it ood rock walls, about ten feet high! Waterfalls gushed off the rocks into the ond. The beautiful golden sun (which was beginning to set) came shining rough a clearing of trees. It was magnificent!

t's a billabong!" I cried.

Good, we can come and bathe here!" said Mollie, pleased, "We'll come back ere once we've unloaded the tent and the emergency box".

But something stopped our plans and we wouldn't be able to visit the llabong that day!

CHAPTER FIFTEEN

A SHOCK

We stood at the water's edge and looked across the beautiful billabong.

The water was a beautiful dark green with splodges of paler green here and there. The waterfall made a terrific noise and behind it we could see little hidden caves with stalactites drooping down!

"Look, there's a pheasant!" called Mollie, and sure enough there was a beautifi young pheasant taking a sip from the water.

"Woof!" barked Snowball from behind us. We all turned around and saw that Snowball had found the bones of a dead bird!

"Don't eat it!" said Ava, but Snowball knew she wasn't allowed to eat bones i case they punctured her gums.

The bones were old and dry - no stain of blood could be seen anywhere. I took the skull and popped it into my pockets. I like collecting animal skulls - o course, I only take them from already dead animals!

"See those rocky ledges up there?" said Ava, "On a fine day, we could dive of into the water, if it's deep enough!"

"What a great idea!" I said, "We'd better get back home now, it's quarter to seven and the sun's already setting!"

So we grabbed our things and continued on our way.

We passed small streams and found lots more berry bushes which we feaste on.

Eventually we found the coast. We turned left and followed it. We were soc at our lovely 'C' shaped beach.

"Bobby, QUICK! Something has happened to our house!" Ava shouted.

Mollie and I ran over. There lay our house, but some of the sticks/poles had been smashed away and our whole roof had fallen in! This made the walls bulge out!

"Looks as if someone else IS here!" said Mollie.

"It wasn't a human who did this" said Ava, "Look!"

We saw, leading away from the house, a trail of animal tracks!

"Which animal do these tracks match?" said Ava. I knew so I said, "They're crocodile...crocodile...what are crocodiles' feet called? Flippers? Paws? Feet? Anyway, whatever they're called, a crocodile has been here!"

"Woof!" barked Snowball, saying that she could SMELL crocodile in the air!

"It looks like he's a biggen too!" cried Mollie, studying the 'paw prints' carefully.

The crocodile certainly had knocked our house about. In the end we put up our tent to live in until we rebuilt the official abode.

"We must understand" I said, when we were all sat round the fire eating supper, "We must understand that we aren't dealing with a character out of a children's story. No - this is a REAL crocodile which can eat humans".

I seemed to become captain after that. I started giving out orders and rules.

"We must find out where this animal lives before anything else" I said, "Is that clear?"

"All clear" said the two girls.

"We must then make our house as far away from the crocodile as possible, and up inside a tree. All clear?"

"All clear"

“If any of us are to come face to face with the croc we are to run home and tell everyone where you met the croc so we know to avoid that area - all clear?”

“All clear”

“None of us are to harm the crocodile on any account. All clear?”

“Clear”

“Right!” I said, “We set out tomorrow on a croc hunt! Let’s go to bed!”

We crowded into the dark green tent and turned on a spotlight which was taken from the emergency box.

The tent had two bedrooms at the back and a front room where there were four windows! I shut all the ‘curtains’ and retreated to my bedroom. Mollie and Ava were in one bedroom and Snowball and I were in the other! Both bedrooms were divided by a flimsy white sheet of some sort, which could easily be pulled aside to talk to each other.

I lay awake worrying about the crocodile, when Mollie’s head appeared around the ‘curtain’.

“Bobby” she whispered.

“I’m awake” I said.

“I’ve been thinking” said Mollie, “Couldn’t the crocodile live in that billabong we found today?”

“Possibly” I said, “We’ll have a good poke about tomorrow”.

CHAPTER SIXTEEN

THE CROC HUNT

That night was the first night that I didn't sleep deeply but at least I had SOME sleep - right?

The next morning, before setting out on a crocodile hunt, we moved our tent into a more shady area, for inside it was very stuffy - you could hardly breathe!

We found a nice patch under some bendy wych elm trees! We had to do a lot of shoving to get the tent under though, but finally managed it!

"It's VERY cosy in here!" said Ava, "The leaves of the tree give a dim, green glow in here".

"It's perfect!" exclaimed Mollie.

We then set out on the croc hunt! We took a pocket full of berries with us to solve hunger problems.

"Should we try the billabong?" said Mollie.

"Yes" I said, "We said we would".

We changed our direction towards the beautiful billabong area. We saw plenty of deer all the time.

"They seem awfully talented at looking after themselves" said Ava, "They're as plump as can be!"

"You're right!" said Mollie, "Maybe it's because it's a grassy area".

"Or somebody feeds them" suggested Ava.

“Why would someone want to keep millions of tame deer on a small island?” said Mollie.

“Plenty of reasons” I said, “Some people - believe it or not - like to raise innocent animals to maturity just to have a game of shooting!”

“But SURELY the deer don’t know how to use a gun!” said Mollie, startled.

“Of course not” said Ava, “The humans shoot the deer!”

“I simply do not believe you” said Mollie.

“It’s true” I said sadly, “Some humans are just evil...well...it’s the devil really”.

“Well if people are raising these poor deer to be shot” said Mollie, “that means people do come here!”

“Well, it was only a theory” I said.

We rounded a corner and found ourselves at the billabong! But we were at the top of the waterfall, not at the bottom like yesterday!

Everything looked different up from where we were. Everything seemed stretched! The view stretched down in front of us!

“We’ll sit on the edge and watch for crocodiles whilst eating our lunch” said Ava. We sat down on some soft grass next to the mighty waterfall.

We all knew the croc hunt was going to be long - crocodiles don’t come and show themselves to the world - they would rather be a ‘has been’ than a ‘bean’.

“What’s that over there?” suddenly said Mollie pointing behind us. We saw a WHOLE carcass of a deer!

Snowball was sniffing it but wasn’t eating it. She knew that the bones may puncture her throat and was aware of it.

“The croc must have got it” I said, “Look at the bite marks”.

“Ah, well” said Ava, “It’s nature’s way”.

That doesn't mean it isn't upsetting though" said Mollie.

We returned to our spot and continued to watch for crocs. Once we thought e saw one but it was just a log floating by.

Ve'll wait till night" I said, "If we still haven't spotted one we'll hunt mewhere else tomorrow. We simply must..."

THERE'S ONE!" screamed Ava. We looked. At first we couldn't see anything ut then we managed to pick out the camouflaged body of the crocodile. He was etending to be a huge black rock. He was sitting on the shore of the billabong atching us with two bright, yellow eyes!

But oh, how huge he was. He was MASSIVE. He was GIANT! He was at ast thirteen feet in length!

Ava was dancing about on our ledge screaming, "Can't you see him, he's UGE. Look at him, he's..."

Ava, look out!" I yelled. Ava had tripped over a tree root that stuck out of the ound like an arch. I lunged forward to grab her but she fell!

With an almighty SPLASH Ava disappeared into the green water on which e waterfall plunged!

CHAPTER SEVENTEEN

THE CROCODILE

As soon as Ava hit the water the crocodile (who was watching everything from the shore) dived in and began swimming over to the white froth left from Ava' fall!

Snowball began to bark furiously at the scaly, dark creature gliding over the water!

Ava's hand appeared out of the billabong. She looked quickly and spotted the huge beast charging at her! She began swimming to the shore as fast as she possibly could - but the crocodile was gaining VERY quickly. I made the biggest quandary in my life. I threw off my hat and dived into the deep, cold billabong water!

When I popped my head out of the water I saw that the croc was still after Ava. He hadn't fallen for my distraction. I opened my mouth and began baa-in like a sheep in pain. I also splashed wildly.

"Baaa-aa!" I screamed, "Baa-baa-aaaa-BAAAA-AAA!!!"

My voice was muffled by the water I was throwing about! But thankfully th croc thought I was a drowning sheep and began charging at me!

I waited till I saw Ava climb safely onto the billabong bank and then I start swimming to the opposite shore!

Unfortunately, the croc caught up to me and tried to bite my leg (did you know you can actually hear a crocs' jaws come together?) SNAP!

Thankfully only my dark blue trousers were bitten - the crocodile grabbed my trousers and pulled them (along with me) down fully under the water!

I waited for the crocodile to head-thrash (that is where the animal thrashes its head so quickly from side to side so that its victims' bones are cracked!), but before he could, Mollie decided to give us a helping hand. She picked up my hat and threw it down like a frisbee - it landed, slap on the croc's eyes!

The croc immediately let go of my trousers and I swam quickly and this time reached the side!

Crocodiles (in case you didn't know) calm down at once if you cover their eyes! That - my readers - is a true fact discovered by Steve Irwin (if you know who he is).

Soon we were all together again standing on the shore of the billabong! My hat (which the croc had ignored after finding out that it was inedible) drifted over and I was able to pick it up again.

I slipped the soggy hat over my head and laughed, "We now know where the croc lives!"

CHAPTER EIGHTEEN

THE STORM

The next day we gathered our things and made off as far away from the billabong as possible!

We found a nice comfortable spot behind a wall of fir trees. There was also a nearby berry bush which would be quite useful.

We had the view of the sea and a nearby sunny beach, but the place where our tent was nice and shady!

Three days passed. We went on walks, rummaged for food, went bathing in the sea and sometimes went to visit the crocodile in his billabong!

But something strange happened one morning after we had all eaten our breakfast (roasted berries). It was quite a windy day, with grey skies above!

The sea was what you would call 'choppy' and all the fir trees were blowing about making a rustling sound!

We were all hidden inside the tent chatting.

"I'm glad those fir trees are hiding us" said Ava, "If they weren't there we'd probably get blown right away!"

"We certainly would" I said.

We were sat in the 'front room' where we had four windows made of plastic. We had fully zipped down the door so the wind couldn't get in. Even so, it could still get in through the gaps at the bottom, which was a great nuisance.

"The wind seems to be getting worse" said Mollie. Indeed it was. Great waves as tall as a car began pounding up the beaches and the palm trees were bending over until their top branches almost touched the floor!

“You know what I’d love to do?” I said suddenly, “I’d LOVE to go outside and feel what it’s like. Who’s coming with me?”

“I’ll come!” said both the girls.

“Woof!” cried Snowball.

We unzipped the door a little bit and stepped out! The wind slapped us hard! There was actually a sharp slapping sound as I stepped onto the beach!

SLAP! Ava came out of the tent. SLAP! Mollie had done the same!

Then there came a kind of muffled slap as Snowball stepped out! We all gasped and gaped in the furious storm!

Just then the wind grew to it’s very highest. Mollie and I promptly fell over into the sand! A HUGE wave as tall as a garage swept over us but it thankfully didn’t take us away out to sea!

There suddenly came a groaning, creaking sound from behind our tent. We shot our heads round and saw an ENORMOUS fir tree beginning to snap! It then came crashing down next to the tent (thankfully not hitting it) and landed heavily!

After that the wind began to settle down a bit! We were quite able to breathe again - though not properly.

We rushed back into the tent and sat down again.

“Don’t you think it’s a bit worrying?” asked Mollie.

“No - why?” Ava and I said.

“Well” said Mollie, “What if another tree falls on top of our tent?”

“No what-ifs” I said at once, “What-iffing is a nasty habit. It only causes a problem”.

After about three hours, the storm had COMPLETELY disappeared! The sky was blue with no clouds! The sea was a light blue. No one could have even guessed that there had even been a storm!

“There isn’t a single breeze!” Mollie exclaimed.

We unzipped the tent and went out into the hot sun. We immediately looked behind us to look at the fallen fir tree!

We saw quite a sight.

CHAPTER NINETEEN

THE TOWER

‿ook” Mollie shouted suddenly. She was pointing behind the wreckage of the llen down fir tree. The tree had revealed a new patch of rocky coast we hadn’t en before! We could all see now what Mollie was pointing at - on a high ound of rock overlooking practically the whole of the island was a tall, round hite tower!

It was definitely built by man. No animal could build a tower on top of a ck and paint it white!

Vhat is it?” Mollie was saying, “Who put it there? I thought you said no man s ever been here, Bobby?”

That’s what I thought” I said helplessly, “But it looks as though SOMEONE AS been here! Besides us!”

‿et’s go and explore it!” said Ava, excitedly.

Ve sure will” I said, “First we’ll pack a snack!”

We packed a bunch of roasted berries left over from that night’s supper and uffed them into our pockets!

We then set out towards the mysterious tower! As we grew close, we could e some of the nearer details of the building. It had an extension part with one indow. The main tower had four windows and a cone-like roof, out of which uck two small chimneys.

There were stone steps leading to the front door which was about five feet ll and was painted light brown...or nougat!

We began climbing the tall steps and soon reached the top. We all expected e door to be locked but when I tried the handle, the whole thing opened easily!

Inside the bottom room was a small table and chairs. On the walls (which were curved to follow the shape of the tower and were painted pale-blue) were hung millions of tiny picture frames each with a unique photo inside!

To the left was another door (painted yellow) which led into the extension and to the right was a set of stairs that spiralled upwards.

“Bobby, look at this picture!” cried Ava, bending down to look at one of the tiny picture frames that was almost touching the floor. In the picture a man wa proudly holding a dead, baby deer up by its legs!

The man was tall and bald. He wore a pair of matching trousers and jumper painted like leaves to help camouflage against the greenery, like the clothes soldiers used to wear during World War Two. He had a black beard which was very long, almost down to his waist. He only had one eye though he wore a ki of eye patch like pirates did (or were rumoured to).

As we looked at the next picture we saw a short, little dwarf-like person trying to hold up an adult deer which was dead. The dwarf had spiky red hair but no beard. He wore the same as the last man (though of course in a smaller version). He was also looking proud like the last man.

Soon we noticed that all the millions of little picture frames held photos of these two men showing off dead deer!

“What IS this all about?” said Ava, confused. She was mad at seeing so many dead animals.

“Don’t you know?” I said, “Those two men are hunters!”

“How DARE they!” said Mollie.

“Can’t you see?” I said, “On some of these pictures these men are carrying guns! I bet they own this island and use it to breed deer so at some point they can come here and shoot them down. They then take pictures and hang them a up here. This is the best shooting tower anyone could ever have! And I bet tho men...”

“Bobby!” screamed Ava, “Look at this photo. That man isn’t holding a deer...it’s something else...what is it?”

“I know what it is!” said Mollie, “It’s a lynx!”

Sure enough, in the tiny photo frame was a picture of the tall, bald man holding up a beautiful lynx triumphantly by its tail.

“Are they also breeding lynx, then?” said Ava.

“No, of course not” I said, “That lynx was hunting ‘their’ deer, so they shot that down too!”

“The cruelty of some humans!” shouted Ava.

We now began finding other small pictures of the two men holding predators instead of deer!

The pictures of predators were of;

Golden Eagle,

Lynx,

Crocodile,

Porcupine,

Python, and even a lion!

“The horrid beasts” said Ava (meaning the humans, not the animals).

We peeped into the extension part and saw a bunk-bed up against the right hand wall. There was also a small fridge with a microwave on top.

“Their living quarters!” I said.

We went back into the picture room and climbed the stairs.

We were in a small, round room with two windows - one looking out to sea and one looking over the rest of the island. Both windows had a large hole in it.

“For the guns, probably” said Mollie, “I wonder where they keep their guns”.

“There they are” said Ava, pointing to the wall. On a rack hung two big rifles!

Without a word, Ava walked over and picked both off their racks! She ran downstairs and we followed - including Snowball.

Ava went over to a rock outside. She put a gun down and raised the other in the air.

“No, Ava!” I cried, “You can’t break someone else’s things!”

“Those men broke all those animals’ lives!” Ava replied - and with that, she brought the gun down with a crash on the rock. She raised it again and brought it down with another crash! CRASH! CRASH! CRASH - CRASH!

By the time my cousin Ava had finished, the gun was just a battered up stick! It couldn’t possibly be used again - Ava picked up the other gun and smashed that one up too! She then went back into the tower and hung the wrecked weapons on their racks!

“At least I’ve saved a few animals” Ava said, “and YOU tried to STOP me, Bobby!”

CHAPTER TWENTY

LETTERS

We climbed up to the top floor of the tower and found a large chest of drawers. We opened the top drawer and saw it was full of paper, each with some tiny writing on it.

"They're all letters!" said Ava, "The men must write letters to each other! Let's read one!"

I picked out a small letter and read it out loud. It said the following;

"Dear Kevin,

I came to the island last Winter and found a lynx prowling around after our deer - I took my gun and killed it - sorry you weren't there but I couldn't be bothered coming all the way back to tell you and then coming back here to find all our deer eaten.

Alice."

"So, there's Kevin and Alice" said Ava, "They must be those men we saw in the pictures! I wonder which is which?"

"Easy!" said Mollie, "We found that picture of that really tall man holding that dead lynx! He must be Alice".

"And the other is Kevin" I said, "That little dwarf!"

"Read another letter!" said Mollie.

"Wait!" I said, "Look, isn't that a letter on that sofa?"

Sure enough, on a pale green couch next to a window lay a small envelope! I picked it up and opened it. I read it aloud. It said;

"Dear Alice,

I visited our island about three weeks ago and found traces of a crocodile - I couldn't find it though, but am going to arrive soon. Please let me shoot the creature. Don't go bustling after it yourself!

Don't worry about the low supply of milk in the fridge. I'm bringing some more with me!

From Kevin".

"This is urgent!" screamed Mollie, "They're going to shoot the crocodile we found in that billabong!"

"Oh no they're NOT" said Ava, "We shall stop them!"

"First of all," I said, "Why would two men send each other letters when the letters are being sent to the same building?"

"Easy" said Mollie, "The men don't live here, right?"

"Right!" we said.

"So one of the men takes a trip here sometimes when he's in the mood for shooting" said Mollie, "And whilst he's here waiting for an animal to stroll by he writes a note for the other man to read when he comes!"

I put the letter back into the envelope and popped it onto the couch.

"So this letter is their next plan?" I asked.

"Precisely!" said Mollie, "All we have to do is stop them from shooting the poor croc".

"We already have stopped them!" said Ava surprisingly, "Don't you remember, I smashed up both their guns! They can't shoot a single animal!"

"Good for you!" I cried happily, "I'm glad you didn't follow my advice and leave those weapons alone!"

CHAPTER TWENTY ONE

EXPECTING THE MEN

'e left the tower and went back to our tent.

Ve must hide our tent!" I said, "If one of the men come back they'll easily ıd us. We don't want that - they'll immediately know who vandalised their ecious guns!"

So that very next morning we shoved our tent right underneath a large low-anched stag's horn sumach. No one could possibly know that a tent was dden there. The tent was also dark-green, so that was a good camouflage!

We scrambled inside and zipped up the entrance. We sat down on the floor ıd began talking.

Ve don't know when to expect the men" said Ava, "All we know is that they ean to come here!"

'es" I said, "And we need to hide and not let them know we're here".

Why not?" said Mollie, "They could take us back to the mainland!"

ou've got a point there" I said.

We could just..." began Ava, but Mollie interrupted.

Wait!" she said, "I think I've got it!"

'ou think you've got what?" I said.

\ plan!" was the reply, "We could write them a letter! We could tell them that e need help!"

No, I don't think that would work" said Ava.

"Nor do I" I said, "The men could easily catch us! Or something like that!"

"But they aren't after us" said Mollie, "They're after the deer!"

"That's true" I said, "But what if..."

"See!" cried Mollie, "No what ifs, that's what YOU said!"

"Fine, we'll do your plan" I said unwillingly, "What exactly is it?"

"I'll tell you" said Mollie, "We go off as soon as we can to the tower and find some paper - they must keep some there because they have to write all those letters to each other - we write on the paper saying we are stranded here and need rescuing. We also say we can meet the next day if they sail their boat (presuming they have one) round to our first beach and shine a light. We'll be waiting on shore. We will then flash a light ourselves so they know we're ther They can then come and pick us up!"

Mollie took several deep breaths after this long speech.

"Where shall we put the note?" asked Ava.

"In the tower of course!" said Mollie.

"Ah-ha!" I said, "I've also made a plan!"

"Go on!" said Mollie.

"It's this" I said, "When the note is left up in the tower and the men come, I'll creep round the building and listen to what they say".

"Why do you need to do that?" said Ava.

"Don't ask questions" I said, "You followed your instincts when you smashed up those mens' guns and you're mighty glad you did. I need to follow my instincts".

"Go on, then" said Mollie.

"Well, that's it really" I said, "Unless the men say something suspicious. They may see the broken guns and know it was us or they may say that they'll go and fetch more guns to shoot the croc, or..."

"Alright! We get what you mean" said Ava.

"When do we go and write the note?" I asked.

"Now, hurry" said Mollie getting up.

We scrambled back out of the tent and zipped up the door. We then made our way back to the beach. We could then follow the coastline round to the tower!

"Shh!" Mollie said suddenly, stopping us all, "Look over there!"

We saw in the evening light, a young deer wandering about next to a huge black rock...but wait! The black rock seemed to have a pair of gleaming yellow eyes! I then noticed the 'rock' was breathing, and suddenly as if it was stung by a hundred wasps, the 'rock' jumped at the deer, opening large, long jaws showing greenish teeth! The jaws came together! SNAP!

You can all guess who this cunning 'rock' was. It was none other than the crocodile! The same crocodile that lived in the billabong with the waterfall and stalactites!

The crocodile's jaws clamped powerfully shut over the deer's back left leg, then the croc head-thrashed!

Crocodiles are the top predator - the animal at the very peak of the food-chain! They are NOT to be mucked with.

We watched the croc for some time more and then carried on with our journey.

Very soon the tower came into view. We climbed the steps and went in.

In a drawer on the top floor we found pens and paper. Mollie took a big sheet of paper and one of the black ink pens.

She wrote the following:

"Dear Kevin and Alice,

A few days ago, we crashed our helicopter on your island and we've been living on it until help could arrive - please come and take us home to Australia - or you can phone our people to tell them to pick us up. There are three of us altogether (and a dog). You can both meet us on the east beach which is shaped like the letter 'C'. We'll be waiting. Hope you don't mind but we've been eating some of those delicious berries that grow here - love the island and its wildlife (would make a great nature reserve).

The Three Islanders".

"That will do, won't it?" said Mollie.

"Fine!" I said, "Now go and leave it on the sofa next to the window".

Mollie did as she was told.

"Now let's get out of here and watch for the men" I said, "We should be expecting them soon".

CHAPTER TWENTY TWO

OUR WAITING PAYS OFF

Once back inside our tent we didn't quite know how to continue with our plan.

"We don't know when the men will be here" said Ava, "So how are you, Bobby, supposed to creep to the tower? You can't go before the men get here because they'll see you".

"I know" I said, "We'll just have to see how everything happens".

"Well" said Mollie, "Whatever happens NO animal is being harmed".

"Of course - of course" Ava and I said together.

We bedded down and fell asleep at ONCE!

In the morning we went for a walk. It had rained heavily during the night and everywhere was damp and muddy!

We decided to walk to the crocodile's billabong for a day out.

When we got there everything seemed different. The sides of the water were slippery and muddy and some mud had sludged down into the water!

Over the other side we could all clearly see the crocodile perching in a muddy patch.

"Did you know?" I said, "Crocodiles LOVE mud?"

"Yes - we did" said Mollie.

"Steve Irwin says they are 'masters of mud'!" I continued, "They can hold their breath for AGES and can dig deep down into the sticky, slimy mud!"

“They’re incredible animals - really” said Ava, “Though most people don’t see it that way”.

“No” I said, “They just think of boots, handbags and belts when they see a croc”.

“Horrible” said Mollie. Everybody agreed - even Snowball who gave the most agreeable “Woof”.

As it grew dark we set off back home. On the way we found another berry bush and we picked some.

We reached the coast and began to follow it home. About half way home we heard the sound of a motorboat.

“It’s the men!” I cried, “Quick, run back to the tent!”

We charged back home, but only the girls and Snowball went in - I had to carry out our plan and spy on the two men!

I rushed on to the tower. All the time I could hear the motorboat chugging along!

I reached the steps at the bottom of the tower and raced up!

I then crept round to the back of the tower and hid behind a bush! It was now about six o’clock and the sun was beginning to set.

I caught a few glimpses of the motorboat as it sailed over to a flat kind of beach at the bottom of the hill on which the tower sat.

When the boat reached land two figures got out and pulled it to a tree. They tied it to the tree.

The two figures were definitely the two from the tiny pictures on the wall in the tower - one was very tall and the other was like a dwarf!

The men bounded up the stairs and went into the tower - the door shut with a bang.

I began to climb up the wall of the tower. The walls were old and dented so ere were lots of little holes for my feet.

I actually managed to climb all the way to the cone-shaped roof! The top ndow was open so I could hear perfectly - I held onto the two chimneys for ar life.

I couldn't hear the men at first. They were obviously making some food - I pt hearing the clanks of cutlery but eventually they came upstairs and I heard rfectly. This is what they said:

Iere's that letter you wrote"

'es, but what's this?"

nother letter"

)id you write it?"

)f course not - did you?"

hut up. I wouldn't have asked you if I had written it"

.et's read it"

will"

And then one of them began reading the letter which Mollie had written. I ard a few gasps from the other man and then talking:

Vhat shall we do?"

'ake these 'islanders' home of course"

3ut what about the croc? He'll eat our deer!"

'ome on, let's go and shoot the croc and then rescue these trespassers. What d they want to crash their helicopter here for?"

I heard the men rush downstairs and then I heard some horrified screams!

"Our guns!"

"They're battered to pieces!"

"Who did this?"

"Don't you know?"

"No"

"The trippers of course!"

"I'll knock 'em out for this"

"Me too, come on. We'll get our other guns from the boat".

CHAPTER TWENTY THREE

ON THE BEACH

I slid down the tower wall and rushed back to our tent, slipping as I went because the ground was wet and soggy and 'squidgley'.

I decided to run the long way round to our tent because I wouldn't meet the two men.

Very soon I was back inside the tent being kicked by Snowball's tongue.

"What happened?" asked Ava, "Did the men say anything? Did you hear anything?"

"I sure did!" I said, "Both the men guess one of us smashed their guns and they said they're going to knock us out".

"Whew" said Mollie, "I'm glad you were listening - we could have all been knocked out".

"What else did they say?" asked Ava.

"They said," I said, trying to remember, "I could hardly hear the last bit because the wind was blowing in my ear, I think I heard them say they'd get their other guns from the boat".

"So they CAN shoot that crocodile!" cried Ava, "They've got more guns!"

"You're right!" I said.

"We have to stop them!" cried Mollie.

"What's our plan?" said Ava.

I racked my brain for an idea.

"I think I've got one" I said, smiling, "Yes, I think I certainly have".

"Go on" said Ava, "What is it?"

"Well..." I began, but stopped when I heard something, "What was that?"

The noise came again - much louder.

"Where are you? We heard you!"

"It's the men" I whispered quickly.

"They'll see us" panicked Mollie.

"Sit still" I whispered, "They won't find us if we're quiet - we're too camouflaged".

So we fell into silence and listened to the men outside who were scrambling about in the leaves.

"Let's just go to the beach and wait for 'em" said one man.

"But I distinctly HEARD them" we heard the other say.

"You imagined it" came the first man's voice, sounding cross.

After that they must have left because we didn't hear anything more.

"It's safe" said Ava, "They've gone".

"Woof!" barked Snowball, saying that the men had well and truly gone.

"So, what was your plan, Bobby?" said Mollie.

"I've completely forgotten it" I said, trying to remember, "It's no good, I've lost it".

"Now it's MY turn to make a plan" said Ava suddenly, "I've been wanting to do it ever since I heard about those men".

"Go on" Mollie and I said, and Snowball made an impatient noise.

"Let's go straight to the 'C' shaped beach and show those men what we're made of" said Ava, "Come on, if you're not coming, I'll go myself".

"Wait!" I cried, but Ava interrupted.

"No waiting" she said, "I'm going".

She unzipped the tent-flap and scrambled out - Mollie and I decided not to desert her and we followed.

I found a strong stick and took it with me, using it as a hiking-pole (I like doing that sort of thing).

At one point, Mollie slipped into a puddle full of clay. When she brought her foot out it was covered in the pale-brown stuff which began to harden at once!

We soon found the 'C' shaped beach. We could see the ruin of our first home, a pile of sticks and parachute cloth.

There was no sign of the men. We could hardly see for it was already dark.

"Where are..." began Ava, but as she spoke a dark figure leaped out from behind a bush and clasped her tightly with both arms!

Another dark figure (though smaller than the other) lunged out at me but I swung my 'walking pole' right into his head.

CRACK!

The dark figure backed away, holding his head with both arms. I saw him trip over a stone and crash to the ground. Ava was struggling with the other, bigger man.

I decided I wasn't going to have this. If there was going to be someone in control of the scene it was going to be me...

CRACK!

I brought my stick down onto the tall figure's hand so hard that he dropped Ava at once!

"ENOUGH OF THIS!" I boomed, "LET'S BE CIVIL!"

CHAPTER TWENTY FOUR

LOTS OF THINGS HAPPEN

hen both the men realised I had taken control of the scene, they subsided at ce, though the tall guy didn't stop rubbing his hand.

Vhat did you want to grab me for?" asked Ava, innocently.

'ou know why" said the small man gruffly - he fished into his pocket and ought out a torch. He switched it on and examined us all.

Ve thought you were all adults" said the tall man. He decided to be friendly - r he saw that he wouldn't get anywhere by being rough.

Ava suddenly spotted the small dwarf like man shifting something under his m to the other - it was a rifle!

Without a second thought, Ava kicked the barrel and sent the weapon high to the air. The man gave a shout and reached out for it but Ava (who was sily taller than him) caught it and threw it at a rock where it cracked!

Vhat did you do that for?" cried the tall man, "That's our property!"

)o you both have a gun licence?" I intervened.

They both looked at me astounded, then looked at each other.

'...yes" said the dwarf, "We d...do".

Vhere is it then." I said. The men went red. The tall man took a small card out his pocket and showed it to me.

hine the light on it" I said. They did as I asked.

I saw that the man was holding a pale-purpley-white card with a picture of him on it. There were some words next to the picture that said:

"Alice's Driving Licence - passed on May the Fourth (be with you) 1942"

"That's a driving licence" I said, "Not a gun licence"

"Same thing" the man said, putting the card back into his pocket.

"For your information..." I said, taking off my hat and throwing it to the floor, "...driving licences and gun licences are NOT the same thing, and as children suggest not to brandish one".

"Alight - ma!" said the dwarf sarcastically.

I pointed my stick straight at his nose as if I were holding a sword.

"Are you threatening me?" said the man, whose name was Kevin.

I raised the stick a little higher and said softly, "Indeed - I am".

Kevin (who wasn't really an expert on sticks) found a thin branch to use as sword - it was a flimsy stick and I knew it - I slashed my 'sword' hard and the clashed. Immediately the top half of the man's sword snapped off!

"Why don't we just take you home?" said the other man, butting in.

"Well, first of all" said Ava, "Why do you kill the deer?"

"Well, for sport" said the tall man called Alice, "How do you know we kill the deer?"

"Oh, we just know" said Ava plainly.

Suddenly I noticed something. There was a long, black rock nearby which hadn't been there before...and now it began to move...it opened two enormous yellow eyes!

Both the men didn't notice it though. They were facing the other way!

Snowball was the first to do something and that something that she did was to run away. She dashed behind a bush and hid!

The huge rock jumped out at the two men - opening giant jaws! Both men managed to dodge but the 'rock' wasn't going to give up. It dived at them again!

"IT'S THE CROC!" shouted Ava. She began hopping about screaming, "Get them croc, get them, they were going to get YOU, now you can get THEM! Get them, crocky!"

But crocodiles are 'ambush' predators, which means they hide in camouflage until their target wanders by. Ambush predators can move EXTREMELY quickly but can only go a few feet before resting, so if a crocodile misses its prey the first time, it gives up and waits for another.

So the croc returned to its 'rock' camouflage and began waiting for its food.

"Filthy beast" muttered Alice, the tall man.

The two men backed away from the crocodile and beckoned for us to come over. We did as they wanted.

"Follow us. We'll just take you to Australia" said the dwarf, "Alice is phoning your 'people' as you call them, to tell 'em to be ready".

Alice, as we saw, was indeed on the phone to someone and very soon he ended the call.

Both men began to lead us towards the tower and to the place I knew they had tied up their boat.

"I'll take another gun up and shoot the croc before we go" we heard one of the men say, "I left three NEW guns in the boat".

CHAPTER TWENTY FIVE

A MIRACLE

We reached the boat and the men untied it (because it was tied to a tree). Alice reached in and brought out a small shotgun-thing!

“Back in a sec, Kev” he said and rushed back the way he had come!

“He’s killin’ the croc” said Kevin.

We watched in horror as the tall figure of Alice disappeared behind a tree!

Ava couldn’t take it. She dashed after the man but Kevin grabbed her and shoved her backwards!

Just then, Ava had an idea. I could see it in her eyes! She bent down and picked up a rock about the size of your fist when clenched. She hurled it at Kevin’s leg.

CRACK!

We actually heard the cracking of his knee bone! He collapsed into the boat yelling in pain!

All three of us, and Snowball, darted off towards the ‘C’ shaped beach!

“You’re not setting a very good example, Ava” I said.

When we got there we saw the huge black rock (which was actually the crocodile) perching near to a black figure. The figure was Alice. We saw him loading his shotgun!

Quick-as-a-flash, Ava and Snowball ran at him! Unfortunately, Ava’s foot bent into a deep patch of sand and she toppled over but Snowball sprang at Alice and knocked the gun out of his hand!

Ava didn't notice where she had fallen...she didn't notice a large rock next to her opening its jaws...when she finally DID notice it was too late...the crocodile roared out at her and bit her ankle!

A crocodile's jaws are so strong they can crush a bone!

The croc didn't let go of poor Ava's ankle. Instead he began to head-thrash! In the background, Snowball was still fighting with the angry Alice - who was trying to shoot the angry dog!

Just when Ava had given up all hope of life, a miracle occurred. The croc, for some reason best known to God, let go of her ankle and headed off into the wilderness!

The first thing I did was to run to the ruin of our house! I ripped a hunk of the parachute cloth off and ran back to Ava!

I folded the cloth around her ankle as tight as I could but Ava took it off me and tightened it herself!

BANG! A shot sounded from Alice's shotgun!

"You deal with him" Ava choked!

I stood up and walked slowly over to the man and dog. Snowball hadn't been shot. Alice had missed!

"Snowball" I said sternly, "Leave Him".

Snowball left Alice and went over to Ava. I addressed the man on the floor - I looked straight into his eyes and recited a piece out of the Bible (which I call 'God's word'):

"You are a child of the devil and an enemy of everything that is right! You are full of all kinds of deceit and trickery. Will you never stop perverting the right ways of the Lord?"

Saying this had an immediate effect upon Alice. He stood up and began to choke. He couldn't think of anything to say!

Behind Alice stood the huge scaly crocodile! And in one bite, the magnificent animal head-thrashed into the man's legs, breaking them at once! The man tumbled down and with one giant SNAP, the giant croc penetrated straight through his skull! At once the man died!

I took one last look at the human carcass and shrugged my shoulders. I said to myself, "Ah well, it's nature's way" and I then walked back to Mollie and Ava...oh and Snowball!

CHAPTER TWENTY SIX

ALONE AGAIN

ва's ankle was still bleeding. Snowball was licking the sore as most dogs do. ollie had dabbed it a bit with some tissue that she always carried with her.

We wrapped her leg up with the tissue and added the finishing layer using e parachute cloth.

can't walk" she said, "Mollie, you go back and see if Kevin is still at the at!"

Off Mollie scurried with Snowball at her side.

I stayed behind to comfort Ava. We ate some berries we had inside our ckets and really enjoyed them.

The sun began to rise just at that moment! And a vast mist rose up and dew gan to form on the leaves! It was a magnificent sight!

After a time, Mollie returned.

hat dwarf man...what's his name?" she said.

evin" I said.

es, Kevin, well he's gone, motorboat and all!" said Mollie, "What are we pposed to do now?"

Vait for help!" said Ava, "Don't you remember? Alice was on the phone to r family to tell them we were being brought home, so if we don't turn up then ey can come and get us!"

Iow will they know where to look?" said Mollie.

“They can tell the police!” I said, “And the police can track the place where th
phone-call took place!”

“They’ll come straight to us!” cried Ava, “Let’s just sit back and wait for then

So for the rest of the morning we lounged around, exploring parts of the island we hadn’t been to and bathing in the cool sea.

“It was an adventure!” said Ava (she hadn’t been able to move a lot because o
her ankle) “and I STILL ADORE that beautiful crocodile, even though he cou
have killed me - every animal can be loved!”

“I could hardly even tell it WAS an adventure” I said, “I would call it; AN EXPERIENCE OF A LIFETIME!”

“We wanted to find a billabong, didn’t we?” said Mollie, “And we wanted to find a croc, and we found BOTH!”

At about midday, we heard the sound of a helicopter. When we looked we saw a low-flying black helicopter circling the island. It had white letters on the side saying;

POLICE!

We all began waving madly with both arms!

CHAPTER TWENTY SEVEN

HELP ARRIVES

We watched the police helicopter as it began a slow and graceful decent. It was a large helicopter and could fit plenty of people inside!

The helicopter landed on the sandy beach - we had to cover our eyes from the grains of sand that flew everywhere!

The engine was switched off and a few doors opened!

Out came six people. They were;

Two policemen

A doctor

Aunt Julie!

Mum!!

And someone else stumbled out. It was none other than Grandad McCain!

Mum ran forward and clasped me tightly. The tears sprang out of her eyes!

Aunt Julie flung herself on Ava whilst the doctor inspected her ankle.

Of course Mollie had no one to hug so she bent down and clasped her arms around the fluffy Snowball.

Grandad stood in the background looking around in amusement.

"Oh, Bobby!" cried Mum, "What happened? We waited and waited for Thomas' helicopter to arrive but it never came! Where is Thomas?"

The doctor put a temporary cast thing over Ava's ankle and we climbed into the helicopter.

As the helicopter rose we all grabbed our tummies and cried, "Goodbye island, hope to see you again!"

We began to relate everything that happened from the moment we took off in Thomas' helicopter called Betty, up to the part Alice the tall man had his head bitten by the angry crocodile!

"So, so old Thomas is dead?" mumbled Grandad. Nobody answered.

"What happened to you? Mum?" said Ava.

"Well" said Julie, "You left us in Thomas' helicopter and we waited for him to come back. We waited for four hours before Jake rung Grandad McCain to ask if you were there, but he said you weren't! After that we went straight to the nearest police station and reported you missing! Then about two weeks later the police phoned us and said that three children and a dog had been found on a small island!"

"That would have been Alice on the phone" I said, "I thought the person on the other end didn't sound like any of you. It must have been the police".

"So after that..." went on Aunt Julie, "...we got a free ride in the police helicopter to pick up Harriet and Grandad McCain and then the police tracked on their radar a small island! And we found you!"

And that, my dear readers, was the story of my holiday in Australia! But don't worry! The story isn't finished yet!...

CHAPTER TWENTY EIGHT

AFTERWARDS

In case you're wondering, we afterwards found out that recently Thomas had been having heart problems - this is what caused him to faint in the helicopter. Unfortunately, Thomas' body couldn't be salvaged. A few days after leaving the island the helicopter wreck blew to pieces! The only remnants of Thomas himself was a knee bone!

The police helicopter had taken us all to the rest of the family waiting at the camping spot where a minibus was hired to take us all to an airport where we flew all the way back to Barley!

We also found out that the island we crashed on belonged to the National Trust. They were keeping the animals safe! They didn't even know about Alice and Kevin!

When we told the National Trust about the hunters and their tower and how we had saved the living things there, they were so pleased with us that they said we could phone them up any time and they would take us in a helicopter (you can see we're not afraid of helicopters, even after being in a crash) to the island and we could live in the tower that Kev and Alice had built illegally!

Local reports had said that people had seen Kevin and his motorboat moor up at a local harbour and then Kevin was seen boarding a plane for Denmark!

Right now I'm sat in the top room of the little white tower writing the last few pages of my book! I'm using some paper I found in the drawer that Kevin and Alice used to leave their letters to each other!

The island is still teeming with deer and the croc is still living in the beautiful 'billabong' we had found! And, of course, there's no one to shoot him now! We named the croc 'Black-rock' because that's what he looked like!

We called the 'C' shaped beach 'Alice's Demise' as this is where Alice had been eaten! But more often we called the beach 'Meeting beach' because this is where we met with the two men!

Keep on loving animals, no matter what shape of size, ALL can be loved!

Printed in Great Britain
by Amazon